Where Does It Come From?

From Flower to Honey

by Penelope S. Nelson

JOHNSTON PUBLIC LIBRARY
6700 MERLE HAY ROAD
JOHNSTON, IOWA 50131

WITHDRAWN

Ideas for Parents and Teachers

Bullfrog Books let children practice reading informational text at the earliest reading levels. Repetition, familiar words, and photo labels support early readers.

Before Reading
- Discuss the cover photo. What does it tell them?
- Look at the picture glossary together. Read and discuss the words.

Read the Book
- "Walk" through the book and look at the photos. Let the child ask questions. Point out the photo labels.
- Read the book to the child, or have him or her read independently.

After Reading
- Prompt the child to think more. Ask: Bees make honey. Can you think of other foods that come from animals or insects?

This edition is co-published by agreement between Jump! and World Book, Inc.

Jump!
5357 Penn Avenue South
Minneapolis, MN 55419
www.jumplibrary.com

World Book, Inc.
180 North LaSalle Street, Suite 900
Chicago, IL 60601
www.worldbook.com

Copyright © 2021. All rights reserved. No part of this book may be reproduced in any form without written permission from the publishers.

Library of Congress Cataloging-in-Publication Data

Names: Nelson, Penelope, 1994– author.
Title: From flower to honey / Penelope S. Nelson.
Description: Minneapolis: Jump!, Inc., [2021]
Series: Where does it come from?
Audience: Ages 5-8.
Audience: Grades K-1.
Identifiers: LCCN 2019054987 (print)
Jump! ISBN 9781645275329 (hardcover)
World Book ISBN 9780716621157 (hardcover)
Subjects: LCSH: Honey—Juvenile literature.
Bee culture—Juvenile literature.
Honeybee—Juvenile literature.
Classification: LCC SF539 N445 2021 (print)
DDC 638/.1—dc23
LC record available at https://lccn.loc.gov/2019054987

Editor: Jenna Gleisner
Designer: Anna Peterson

Photo Credits: Shutterstock, cover; Slawomir Zelasko/Shutterstock, 1; Fishman64/Shutterstock, 3; Tatevosian Yana/Shutterstock, 4; elmvilla/iStock, 5, 22tl, 23bm; Magdalena Ruseva/Dreamstime, 6–7, 23tr; Diyana Dimitrova/Shutterstock, 8–9, 22tr, 23bl; Nenad Nedomacki/Dreamstime, 10–11 (beekeeper), 23tl; DADIKONNA/iStock, 10–11 (bees), 23tl; Dutchinny/Dreamstime, 12–13, 22mr, 23tm; Kzenon/Shutterstock, 14, 23br; Noble Nature/Shutterstock, 15, 22br; Olha Tytska/Shutterstock, 16–17; Evan Lorne/Shutterstock, 18; sweetOlli/Shutterstock, 19, 22bl; Moyo Studio/Getty, 20–21, 22ml; Tsekhmister/Shutterstock, 24.

Printed in the United States of America at Corporate Graphics in North Mankato, Minnesota.

Table of Contents

Busy Bees	4
From Flower to Table	22
Picture Glossary	23
Index	24
To Learn More	24

Busy Bees

Honey is sweet! Where does it come from?

◀····honeybee

Honeybees!
They fly to flowers.
They eat nectar.

They don't eat it all.

They bring some to their hive.

Honeycomb is inside.
Nectar turns into honey!
Cool!

Who is this?
A beekeeper!
He wears a suit.
Why?
So he doesn't get stung!

He lifts out each frame.

There is wax on top.

wax

He scrapes it off.

The frames go in a machine.

It spins.

Honey pours out.

It goes through a filter.

Why?

To catch more wax.

filter

Then it goes in jars.

jar

We buy it.
We eat it.
Yum!

From Flower to Table

How does honey get to our tables?

1. Bees eat nectar.

2. Bees bring nectar to their hive. They make honey in honeycomb.

3. Beekeepers remove the frames from the hive.

4. They scrape the wax off.

5. A machine removes the honey from each frame. The honey is put in jars.

6. We buy and eat the honey!

Picture Glossary

beekeeper
A person who raises bees.

frame
A structure inside a hive that holds honeycomb.

hive
An enclosed structure that is built to house honeybees.

honeycomb
A wax structure made by honeybees to store honey.

nectar
A sweet liquid from flowers that honeybees gather to make into honey.

wax
A substance made by honeybees that is used to make honeycomb.

Index

beekeeper 11	honeybees 5
filter 18	honeycomb 8
flowers 5	jars 19
frame 12, 17	machine 17
hive 7	nectar 5, 8
honey 4, 8, 17	wax 14, 18

To Learn More

Finding more information is as easy as 1, 2, 3.

❶ Go to www.factsurfer.com

❷ Enter "fromflowertohoney" into the search box.

❸ Choose your book to see a list of websites.